PRAISE FOR MARSTON HEFNER

Debut author Hefner alternates from aggressiveness to vulnerable displays of emotion in this striking flash fiction exploration of romantic relationships, often with illicit or taboo dynamics."

— PUBLISHERS WEEKLY

Equally charming and unhinged, the stories in Marston Hefner's *High School Romance* will twist you into a bundle of giggly nerves.

— BRIAN ALLEN CARR, *OPIOID INDIANA*

Marston Hefner's *High School Romance* is a resounding answer to a pervasive ennui. Contemplative reverie and tactility of thought, that interiority scooped gleefully inside out is his lovesick signature, his lyrical sense of daring, giving passage to a raging river of intrusive thoughts, obsessive preoccupations, shattering stream-of-consciousness memories. A gloriously voluptuous vision, an unbearably hilarious anti-book, a marker as Hefner is an unlikely forerunner in a new kind of confessional.

— MANUEL MARRERO, EXPAT PRESS

Marston Hefner strums the language in tunings all his own. His sentences dare themselves forward and backward into eddies of the purest impurities. No one writes more thunderstrikingly of filiality gone berserk. *High School Romance* is the debut of a vital and long overdue new voice.

— GARIELLE LUTZ, AUTHOR OF *WORSTED*

sordid / neurotic / tramadolian / oedipal / alt lit / nouveau roman / soft sci fi / hard to read / this and not feel / for marston/ his inanity / & all / humanity

— STEPHANIE YUE DUHEM AUTHOR OF
NAME AND NOUN

Hefner writes like a gamer who can walk both worlds, taming a gauntlet of bosses, transcending consoles.

— SEAN KILPATRICK AUTHOR OF
SUCKER JUNE

"Marston has a singular voice cleaved from concentration like the knuckled work of a monk. You will learn about yourself as you delve into these stories."

— ELLE NASH, AUTHOR OF *NUDES*,
ANIMALS EAT EACH OTHER, AND *GAG*
REFLEX

HIGH SCHOOL
ROMANCE

MARSTON HEFNER

CL◀SH

Copyright © 2022 by Marston Hefner

Cover by Matthew Revert

CLASH Books

Troy, NY

clashbooks.com

ISBN: 978-1-955904-05-6

Distributed by Consortium

For Anna, my love.

TABLE OF CONTENTS

HIGH SCHOOL
ROMANCE

THE MOON IS A TAPESTRY, A NIGHTMARE

the moon is a beautiful place. i think youd like it there. there are many beautiful places i could take you. but no matter where you go there you are. you find yourself in that amazing place. so i take you to the moon and there you are. with yourself. and me. and elon. and even though the moon is very beautiful and very white and it glows you wish you were someplace else. someplace where you were not.

so you fuck elon on the moon. his brain brought us here and i dont have elons sexual prowess or brain which is now something you know. i start to make a spaceship in the mess hall with paper cups and string. while you and elon have sex and talk about feelings.

you walk into the mess hall. as im building my ticket out of here. right in front of me you say elon fucks incredibly well and teaches you life lessons you wouldn't have otherwise learned. right as im wondering if ketchup would be useful. "elon musk has a bigger dick. its also taller. its better." and i tell you stop being mean. i tell you that the things you need to stop are being mean and making me feel so lonely. i tell you i rescued you from the hate of the world. and i expected a sanctuary with you. and now i feel like an idiot. so the least you can do is be nice to me. because nobody is here but you and me and elon.

and at this you listen. because you hate yourself so you end up making everyone hate you. because you hate yourself. so if elon hates you and you hate me then you'll be left alone. and you know at some point youre going to screw up. and elon will hate you. so youll only have me. and if you dont accept me then youll have no one.

i tell you elon has got to go. i tell you to imagine all the things you love in front of you. your books. your music. your orange light bulbs. now imagine my face ripping through them. taking center stage. my smiling face. and that i have a boner. and that, my penis being the new thing you love. being the survivor/murderer of your other favorite things.

you say youd like to watch a horror movie with me. i say sure. i like horror movies. we watch a horror movie in the space station's theater room and elon comes in. i pause the video and stare at him. to let him know we dont want him here. he asks if he could speak to you and i say you're a bit busy at the moment. and i return to the horror film . but elon is autistic and he doesnt know we want him to leave. he also doesnt understand what rejection is. so he says he wants to speak to you over the movie speakers. whose volume is very high. i turn off the movie again. i tell him i'm very glad he brought us to the moon. we love it, we really do. its so beautiful seeing the earth from the viewing room. and the stars are much brighter and bigger here. there are a lot of good things about the moon and i could go on about all of them for a couple of hours. but we're busy watching a movie. a horror movie. which is something we both enjoy. i tell him that the most important thing is that we dont want him around. that you don't belong to anyone anymore.

elon looked confused. he stood at the viewing room door and said nothing. to help him understand i compared your situation to space. i said that no one owns space and thats what a woman is. thats what you are. and it was a really bad metaphor because elon said. i own space. i didnt know how else to explain it. so i said you werent anyones anymore. you were free. just like the sky. no one owns the sky. and you and i were watching a horror movie. and we didnt want him watching it with us. because he didnt like horror movies anyways.

elon musk says i better leave. i stand up and move slowly towards him. then i move fast to throw him off guard. i go to kick him but elon dodges. much faster than i thought he could. i took taekwondo when i was a child but it looked like elon took it just before he left for the moon. i knew elon was going to make me look like a fool. with one really fast punch he knocked me in the face. and my head richocheted back. and then i guess elon put his whole weight into a kick that hit my stomach and made me topple over. he said he didnt want me on his space station anymore. he said he was the owner of space. and you went over to him and he held your waist. you wrapped both your arms around him. so both of you were looking like a power couple with me on the ground. i didnt feel like crying. i just wanted to get out of there. because i looked so silly. i wish you understood that i had barely practiced taekwondo. and that my values didnt encompass self-defense anyways. i was more of a mental dominator. and i wished that we agreed on that. the way we agreed with horror movies. but it was clear then. you thought fighting was a very good thing to know.

so i went to earth alone. i went home and i cried in my fathers lap. i didnt have to tell him what happened. what father doesnt have that exact story himself? i put my face in his lap so my face was buried in his corduroys. his hand rested on my head. here is what he said.

he said the world is very big and the moon is small. there are more women on the earth then there are the moon. and when elon and you break up you'll be alone. the world has a lot of women on it. plenty of fish in the sea. i said i only wanted you. i said there was only one fish named you.

my father said that those in pain seek it out. do it to others and to themselves. that it was cyclical. but when you found your self-worth. then youd come down to earth and live a normal life. until then youd get fucked by elon. and do drugs. and get into trouble. and be mean to people. and itd all look cool and fun but you wouldnt be happy. itd be a show. and the pain wouldnt stop. not until you loved yourself.

i gripped his corduroys and cried. because it was cathartic. it felt good because it wasnt my fault. i looked at his lap and saw my tears. i said i love you papa. i said im glad youre always here. and he patted my head. he invited me to stay at his house for as long as i wanted. so i did. i wanted to feel at home. and i did.

MY PRESENTATION

If this video is in any way coming across as "formal" or "scary" I urge you to talk to the other women in the office who aren't Amy. So you're scared? Hell, I was scared making this video! But honey, I made this video, I went right into that sucker called fear and said, "Where do I fucking sign up?" I put my best face on so it could meet your by now blushing little puckered cheeks. I know I know, the hardest hill to climb is the one that is not the highest but the one imagined. Do you hear me dear? That the hardest obstacles are the ones we make up in our very own squat-damned minds? I am no demon, I am no "bad toucher" as Amy has led you to believe. Just ask Carol what I did about her little boy Frank.

Before you commit to an answer, there are some virtues I own and that I want to highlight. There are also some very difficult vices I need to tell you about which specifically have to do with feelings I have for my dog, certain family members, and When I looked at your face and how it made me feel. As to the virtues, I am confident they will wash over any doubts you have once I tell you about the vices. As to the vices, I cannot so confidently say I have them under control. For example, how I felt about your Instagram just yesterday, well I felt an irrepressible urge to holler, yes holler, mouth open esophagus wide, that I loved you and how I so loved you greater than, what was his name, Manuel Marrero despite his multitudinous amounts of postings and flirtations. Like a rabid feral dog, I felt myself to be, tearing through the midnight moon towards my kill, forever protective of you.

I know it is so hard to be young these days and on social media. My 17 year old daughter tells it to me all the time in a kind of whisper / whimper that I've not only told her but also told her mother is unacceptable. She goes, "Why do all of these guys dm me on Insta?" So I now not only understand her but I also understand you. It is *hard* for people like you, ripe in the world, just looking for some sort of direction. It is clear to me that what you need is an older more experienced looking hand to show you the way.

Believe you me I know you've by now checked my daughter's Instagram. You may or may not have noticed the similarities in your blonde bob and the way your lips both quiver in the presence of an authority figure. These similarities, well Tiffany, let these similarities be like oil on water. Let the eery way you both laugh verbosely be the opposite of a wake up call. Let me merely be a lulling feeling of "familiarity" when the time comes for us to consummate our relationship.

If your coworker Amy at any time mentioned anything related to a supposed "free hands" movement, with me being the leader and sole member, which showed a lot of promise despite the misunderstandings, know that she, Amy, has struggled with mental illness. Because I am privy to such information and because we have gotten so much closer since the beginning of this video, I will make you privy to this information, that Amy started the rumor just after a very long and gruelling company outing involving numerous trust exercises with many hands all over everyones' parts. Her HR representative Dan, I just call him Danny, has told me that after the trip Amy not only refuses to stop washing her hands but is also terrified whenever hands come near her. You of course know my hands are rather large and so an obvious target for Amy's neurosis.

As you watch this, I encourage you to bring this to your best girlfriend. Ask her, in all honesty, if I would make a good fit in your life. Pontificate with her if my brain is wrinkled enough to guide your very youthful and exuberant frame through not only this ruthless workplace but the magical nights of disarray youth get into these days. Get a differing opinion, perhaps from someone older that you trust, a father figure comes to mind, and ask him what kind of man makes for a good husband. I bet you he will say "wisdom" for one. You can even come to me, let me soothe those doubts in your head, the ones that go, "His fingers remind me of prunes." Poo poo to the super-ego in your head, poo poo to the naysayers in the workspace, believe in those who have tread this lonely road before, who are saying, "Let my large hands guide your fresh and nubile face towards a promising and lucrative future."

MY SPECIAL CREATURE

I thought my boyfriend Richard went to Portugal for his extra-curricular sight seeing trip but he's speaking in Spanish. The College Vacation Trip? Richard gets A's with ease and I look at his essays he hangs on his wall. Those fucking A's are going to take you places baby. An A man can always have me because I deserve an A man.

The other night I couldn't kiss him. We watched a movie and he closed his eyes, squinting at the screen. I felt physical about it. But these are just thoughts. We are not our thoughts and we are not our feelings. Unclear what we are but I'm sure it's very good. We are not our thoughts. We are vaginas.

I know I can't depend on him for happiness or self-worth. That's up to me. So what if my organs itch? Over time I am sure something will change. He'll know to put an extra blanket over me when I sleep in because I require just a little bit more than the average gal. A mind reading ability of sweetness. A blanket on me.

But yeah, I couldn't kiss him when we watched the movie. Why don't I just marry my forty-year-old boss who is twice divorced and has a penchant for dangerous sights? A man who conquers the world by stepping his boots on mountain tops and places a little flag with his company logo at the top. A man who emails his employees the picture of him on the mountain and says, "We're going everywhere. Everywhere together." So it's not just him who climbs the highest peaks but it's us.

"How did you know you were in love with Devin?" I ask Tiffany.

"What was the hat party honey?" says Tiffany.

"I don't remember," says Devin.

I require a thousand suns in my name Richard. All dedicated to warming me. Your space heater is not enough and it is depressing. I am sick of the dampness of your carpet. What does it sweat? Before I go Richard I want you to know that after I break up with you I'll think about how I could have made it work if I had just tried harder. I'll think I just had to grow up a bit.

I look at Devin and say, "Piñata."

He cracks up.

I say, "Café leche. Dulce de mi amigo. Lunar de pronto."

He laughs again.

"I can make you laugh pretty easy kid."

"You have no idea what you said."

"I know exactly what I said."

"Que?" says Devin.

Richard my boyfriend says to Devin in Spanish that there is a dog or he is saying but. I think about it and he is saying but, I think. My High School Spanish teacher took me outside the classroom once and pointed to the test I took. He said, "You wrote dollo for the Spanish word doll." For the whole test I did that. Dollo. Toyo. Sheepo. I didn't know what to say to my Spanish teacher.

My feet were stiff. I held my hand in my hand. I knew it was very funny so I smiled but I knew it wasn't right to smile. I felt hot in the face like tears were coming. For a long time I thought I was stupid because I was stupid in school. For a lot of the time I tried to avoid teachers in hallways. They wanted to talk about something. I poured water on my tits in math class. You can't do that. I grabbed boys asses. That's not allowed. So yeah, I thought I was stupid for a long time.

"Where are we going?" asks Tiffany.

"I think we should just stay here," I say.

We are alone. And it feels good to be alone. When alone I can feel my strength.

"It's only 11 babe," says Richard.

"I suppose you're right," I say.

Just the other day my boss patted my back and said I was doing well. He was making eye contact with me. It was intense because I kept the eye contact. I stared at him not knowing what the eye contact meant to him. Did he always look people in the eyes? Because I didn't. For him maybe it was a standard eye contact conversation. He sees me that way. Promising. He sees me that way. I can get there. He can make me think that an apartment is not about money. That getting guacamole is not about money.

When my boss looked me in the eyes I was thinking about fucking him with a strap on. Like a small one because I care about him. Bending him over and making him say I'm the best shit ever. That he can't even touch my shit. "What is my shit like?" "Your shit is so good I can't even touch it." "Am I impregnating you?" "Yes. I mean I don't know." I go all the way in so he stops thinking. "We are having a baby." I say. "I want a baby."

I want to be alone with myself and cry for a while. I

want to tell you that it's been a long time since I have loved.

That I am not a fish in bed. I do not flop with my hands at my side. But with Richard I am a fish. Is that the real test? Do I flop or do I hold?

"Devin. Are you going out tonight?" I ask. I'm a fucking werewolf. I'll own your night. I'm going to steal your fucking boyfriend baby.

"I don't know. I'm awfully tired," says Devin.

For God's sake. Let it be known. This is my contract. My personal contract I am writing right now. I will wait for him. Whoever he is. Just fucking rad love. Engorged bellies. Laughing because it is good to laugh. Believing that the future has feelings and wants to fuck me again. I want him. And go to hell if you think it's all a dream. I'll get it. I'll go for it. The way I go for it. Flight so erratic. Your head going right through the atmosphere pointing right at the sun. Going up to the sun. Not getting burned. Getting so warm that you fall asleep. Vacations that mean something. Trips to Rome where I hold his hand in public. Trips to Rome where I think the gelato tastes good. Boredom a sign of progress. Creatures in the night leaning into us and creating a small thing in the universe that we go through. The rip we go through and are alone.

"I think I'm going to go," I say.

"Do you want to come over tonight?" asks Richard.

"What did you have in mind?"

He shrugs his shoulders.

IM DONE DELLILO

IF DELILLO HAD A HORSE THAT WAS INTELLIGENT
AND THE HORSE HAD THUMBS AND WROTE
BESIDE DELILO> IF DELOILO TOAGHT THE HORSE
HOW TO WRITE ID BE THE HORS

IM DELILLOS HORSE. WATCH ME WRITE.

IF DELILLO HAD A HORSE INSIDE A VACUUM WITH
NO AIR OR MATTER ID WRITE IN THE VACUUM.
THROUGH THE VACUUM DELILLO CARED ABOUT
MY IMPROVEMENT. I AM HIS HORSE. I AM DON'S
PRIDE AND JOY.

AT THE RACETRACK I WILL BE SO FAST THAT I WIN
MEDALS AND MONEY. THE HORSE WHO WINS SO
MUCH MONEY THAT DON DELILLO WILL BE UPSET.
HE NEVER UNDERSTOOD HIS HORSE. MY FATHER
NEVER UNDERSTOOD ME. BUT ON THE RACE-
TRACK IM UNDERSTOOD. I TRAINED MY MUSCLES
SO MUCH THAT ON THE RACETRACK I AM THE

FASTEST HORSE OF THEM ALL. WHEN I WIN
THEY'LL CALL ME "HUGHES" BUT I

IMMEDIATELY CHANG MY NAME TO Lillard. THE
BIGGEST AND PROUDEST OF ALL THE HORSES. NO
ONE WAS REALLY SURE WHERE I CAM FROEM.
DONE DINILOS VACCUUM IS WHERE I CAME
FROM.

WROTE WITH NOTHING AND NO ONE KNOWING
WHAT I WAS DOING AND OTHERS WANTED TO BE
ON THE TRACK EARLY BUT I LET THEM PASS ME
TRAINING IN THE TRACK IN THE ROOM ALONE
WITH MY MUSCLES GROW TALL. GROW TALL.
NOW I FEEL GOOD. NOW I KNOW WHAT DELLILO
WANTED FROM ME. ASKED OF ME. DID NOT
DEMAND FROM ME. SIMPLY KNEW I WOULD BE.

HIGH SCHOOL ROMANCE

She is 17.

I am 27.

Her father Mark is my best friend. He gives me compliments. It feels like he understands me at the core. It is the kind of friendship that is very hard to find. Her father will soon be my father. Her family will be my family.

After the second meeting she told Mark she thought I was so funny. She thought I could make her laugh for long periods of time with minimal effort on my part. The third time we met I did just that. And her friends laughed and giggled when I did. I thought, like, are you sure? I wanted to say, I'm vulgar but I'm not hilarious. I sent her a short story I had written and oh my God could you please send me that other one you were talking about? She said that, "could you please…" And I thought I could please. Please. Could you please allow me to come over to your house? Tell your parents could you please leave for a while? Could I please make you laugh for a whole night just you and I?

Promise to not assume that this is the one and only truth about my feelings. I had this recurring dream of me devouring her. My favorite color is black and my favorite sweater is my p-coat which is black of course and in this dream I am this. I am sucking in and taking her energy. I am taking her youth.

The fourth time we met she threw a fit because she couldn't find the remote. She threw couch cushions into the air like they were responsible. She yelled at her parents from across the room in a girlish way.

"Why the hell do I keep looking for this thing?" she asked.

"Because you're a masochist," I said.

"That's true about me. I am."

She sat too far away on the couch we both occupied. A couch that would take on a huge amount of importance when I thought about her. A couch that signified home. In the fantasy it was always her laying on the couch with me looking at her from the couch. Her looking at me with that smile.

She didn't find the remote so she showed me a Vine video on her phone.

"You didn't like the video, huh?" she asked.

I shook my head.

One day I told Mark that I liked his daughter.

"You know she's a kid right?" he asked.

I told him I knew of course but I was lying. I knew kids when I saw them and all of Liz's friends were kids but when I saw Liz I saw a woman. And it always terrified me to see her next to her friends because they looked like kids. They had those small faces kids have and those grins kids have since they don't know what real pain is. I'm not saying I know either really, I just know it's fucked with me ever since I've been a real live adult. But the point is that Liz has this smile that is light and I want to call her my little creature. I always look at her eyes for too long and how long can I keep up this thing?

I told Mark I liked her again. But he just says she's a kid and if we were older we'd make a beautiful couple and hold on a second, what did I order?

I look at his drink and I want to tell him again but he's focusing on his coffee which is iced and he asked for it hot. I am emailing her, I want to tell him. I am emailing her and what do you think she thinks it means? He's waving over the waitress.

How true is obsession anyways?

Because I imagine a beach with Liz and me on it. No. To be honest I imagine us, we're always in Mark's house, we're on the couch I mentioned before. It's me and Liz in the living room. We're laying down on the respective sides of the couch. The sun is on her face so I can't see it and her hair looks like it's trapped pieces of the sun inside it. Her nose is frowning and I want to take whatever it is that she sees in me. I want to have it for myself. And if I can't do that, I'd like her to be around me for long periods of time.

The last dinner we had together with the whole family she was wearing those shorts that might as well not exist.

"Who do you like more?" she asked. She always wanted to know how much I liked her. I liked her father the most because our friendship was pure and solid. She was chaos and so she was allocated to number 2 and probably always would be number 2. I felt bad for my number 1 friend because I was really going to fuck with him if I kept feeling this way. Anyways, she asked the question and then pointed to herself. She nodded. Then she pointed to Mark. Then she pointed to her mother Laura.

I don't know what Mark and Laura were doing as Liz pointed back to herself again but the point is that these clear walls came on both sides of Liz and I. She pointed to herself again and nodded slowly. I shook my head and looked at the table.

Her mother said something loud and I came back.

"I'm a man," I said. "Who said I wasn't a man?"

"I think you just said that to yourself," said Mark.

I leaned back in my chair and patted my stomach. Liz showed me more Vine videos on that couch made of a soothing fabric I don't know the name of.

"You didn't like that one either," she said.

"Not really."

Then she showed me a meme. I'm not fit for this world at all.

"You can uber home or you can let me drive you home in 10 minutes," said her mother.

"I have statistics homework," said Liz.

"I guess I'll go home. Liz has work to do and so do I," I sighed.

Liz went off to Coachella that weekend and I emailed her.

"Did you see those walls that came up between us when we had dinner? I'm certain I saw them but was wondering if you did too?"

I sent it off and there was no reply until Sunday and even Sunday I didn't get a reply from Liz. Her mother texted me telling me she no longer wanted to pursue a friendship with me and to not try and contact Liz, Thank you.

I said OK.

"Thank you." She wrote again.

So I guess those walls really were just for me. I guess the more that I think about it it doesn't really make sense at all. That my world was occupied by two. I know Liz didn't see the walls at all but if she had I bet my small mannerisms would have taken on significant meaning. That when I swatted the fly that buzzed around my food she would think it was not just a movement of my hand but me saying "I want to know you."

THE KIND OF LIKE, RUNNING MOTION TOWARDS SOMETHING

The challenge of not having a mother in college was immense but I didn't take her seriously when she suggested attaching herself to my back with one of those fetal strap things. I came back home after college and I think my father enjoyed me being back. I had nowhere to go which suited him nice because he liked having me around. I've heard parents should teach their children how to fend for themselves but my father always had a very large great sword in his study.

"You know what I'm going to do with it?" he asked. He'd swing it around a bit.

In my bedroom I tried to understand why my girl-friend broke my heart. I also wanted to know a little bit more of what I wanted to find. In my bedroom at home with my parents tinkering downstairs with Tupperware I noticed a girl had liked an Instagram photo of mine. I then looked at a photo of her standing in front of a subway car with her tattoos and blue eyes showing.

I wrote her saying, "Put me in a hankie and go achoo and I remove your sickness."

She replied with, "Today I bought a cat and I didn't much care for it."

She was very beautiful. I stared at my wall for a while longer and then I thought this is no way to live, that I was getting to but hadn't gotten to the way to live yet. The way to live was with her, maybe, and we'd spend a good deal of the rest of our lives together. Sleep is spent for most of our lives but she'd come second, time wise. The kind of smiles that say to each other and to ourselves that this is what we came to live here for. We didn't come to live for sleep but we came to live for us and even though people say that's an ugly thing to do we'd come to realize that ultimately it was true and how silly it was what other people thought. And it's like, what we would have was like after falling, the part of catching, of feeling the support holding your body and the looking up into her blue eyes which would be smiling.

In my bedroom I looked at her photo again and I thought maybe her eyes are just the white sclerae that make up all eyes, and her irises just happen to be blue because her mother's eyes were blue, and her pupils weren't looking at me but at the camera. That maybe she's just science.

"Can we meet up?" I asked.

"Yes."

After our first date I could not sleep. I called her phone but she did not answer. The difference between loneliness and being alone has always been negligible to me. To distract myself I went on my laptop.

"It was hard," she said to me in the morning.

"What do you mean?"

"It was hard not calling you last night," she said.

"I called you last night," I said.

"I didn't get your call."

I said, "Hmmm that's weird."

"It was so weird," she said. "Can I see you again? I mean I want to see you again."

I took her to a restaurant. It seemed like her blue eyes like tinted her hair blue. It was all very exciting, the date was, and that night I didn't feel devastated being away from her. The feeling was abdicated since I knew she missed me dearly, my mother probably but more my potential girlfriend is what I meant. She missed me in a dire way that I reciprocated the next day with brief kisses and a soothing of her tattooed bicep.

A few months passed and the overwhelming happy feeling of being around her tampered down. The days became every day and I enjoyed this. We ended up watching a lot of shows about girls putting on make-up and looking at their faces in mirrors while talking to their friends who had their faces in mirrors and they talked about boyfriends but other stuff too. Every night we looked forward to watching the shows and during the day we'd text about it. It was pretty cool, the transition in our relationship.

And yea on the fifth month of basically good feelings she said to me, "You said you'd tell me about the darker stuff about yourself."

I told her what they were of course, being in such a trusting and loving relationship I felt I could.

"Is that all?" She asked.

"Yes. I think so," I said.

"To be honest," she said looking at her lap, "I think we should break up. I've been worrying about it constantly even though I don't want it to come true. The stress reminds me of mid-term exams."

"You being too tired to study," I said.

"The kind of responsibility that you don't want to look at," she said. "Being 21 years old in your dorm room and having the clouds start to come over your building. Everything dreary."

"Running away from the next step," I said.

"The next step being marriage and kids and a domestic life."

"Which," I said, "you told me you did not want, in the past."

"And then I said I did want with you, please note," she said.

"And now it's crunch time."

"Now it's crunch time," she said, "and I've barely studied."

"Knowing tomorrow must come but not wanting it to," I said. "You being unprepared, wanting to sleep in, miss the exam which would lead to an F. But you hoping somehow, emailing that you're sick perhaps, somehow there is a way out of the exam without failing, you hope."

"I realize there are expectations completely outside of study hard," she said. "There are expectations from friends to also excel at being a fun kind of girl. To have fun. The kind of fun with no rules at all."

"And you wake up and you do it," I said. "Over and over again. Until it's no longer about the fun but maintaining the appearance of the fun."

"And even though I know what happens," she said.

"The pressure is too much. Some distance is necessary," I said.

"Yes."

"For how long?"

"I don't know," she said.

"Are you going to tell me when you know?"

"Yes."

"I am not a monster," I said. "I would never hurt you."

"I never said you were a monster."

YOU AND ME AND LIKE, WHERE DO WE GO, AFTER ALL THIS TIME?

I fucked my best most prestigious dog in the world today. Fucking my best dog in the world felt so good. I was at my best when I fucked my dog. No one could hold a candle to my dog when we fucked.

I wanted this story to be great 500 years from now but in 500 years bestiality will be normal. So I failed since the story will read something like:

I fucked my girlfriend. Fucking my girlfriend felt so good. No one could hold a candle to my girlfriend when we fucked.

Well then, forever onwards.

I fucked my girlfriend with greatness in my heart. My girlfriend felt my greatness in my heart when we fucked. My girlfriend felt it so much that she cried. That's how good my fucking my girlfriend was. No one else fucked my girlfriend like that ever before.

No matter how much I hurt when my girlfriend left I was still so great. I was so great because I knew the truth. I knew the truth and my girlfriend didn't know the truth and that's because I was great. Knowing the truth was great and I worked hard in this life. And even though my girlfriend worked the hardest, even though she put so many hours into her career, I was even greater than her.

No matter how great she really was, I knew even more. God told me I was great when I prayed to him and God told me I was great when I put words on the page and God told me that all of my rejections, all of them throughout the whole world had come because I was great. God gave me my secret and my secret was dangerous. Then my girlfriend learned that I had fucked my best dog in the best world and she didn't think that was the greatest thing in the world that I could do.

My girlfriend thought my dog fucking was my problem and thought it was abysmal and she never even told me why no matter how hard I tried to get her to. No matter how many times and how many questions I asked her she never said why she hated me. And no matter how many times and how many arguments I had with her she didn't think I was great anymore.

My girlfriend was so convinced that I was so sick she said I was so sick and she was so tired of being so right that I couldn't even comprehend how sick I really was. She said I was so sick that I should be put in a home where there weren't any animals allowed and there weren't any women allowed and she said not even her own daughter should be allowed and so, because I loved her, I was put there.

And when I went home without an ambulance and I went into my front door without my dog jumping up and down and I went into my room with my television set I said, "This is it Marston, this is the last time you ever fuck something up so bad and forever and if you fuck something up this bad again you will be finished and through and no one will ever love you." So I knew I couldn't fuck it up like how I fucked it up before no matter how much God spoke to me and no matter how many songs he sang into my heart.

I went into my study and I read a book and in between reading the book, and in between flipping the pages, and in between noting the language, I looked at my phone. Even though my dog was gone, I felt my dog on the couch beside me. I felt my girlfriend too. I felt the loyalty of all of them and I felt the passion of them all and even the quiet way my dog watched as I read. Despite all evidence, I knew that they were right there with me.

How did I know? It's because I read so much and I wrote so much. It's because when I wrote I felt God and I felt home and I felt really good at what I did. I felt profoundly good at what I did. I knew the profound and how good it felt and so I let it speak to me. The profound said, "I love you Marston, I love you so much and you are good. You are really special and please don't let other people tell you who you are because other people don't do what you do so well."

I WOKE UP THIS MORNING

and my mother staring at the pot and screaming as bits of her perfumed yellow hair caught the very edges of the flame. And so there's me running outside our complex to grab the fire extinguisher just outside our door.

The extinguisher was locked behind a glass case but I hit the glass case as hard as I could with my very thick coat but no matter how thick the coat the glass pierced. O how the glass pierced with a severely painful pang in my left elbow accompanied by a large glass shard protruding from said elbow. Having no time to think about my now molested fur coat, I screamed and I ran which was synchronized to my mother's screaming and running (you know how mothers and daughters are) as my neighbor shouted something to my father who was in my neighbor's very own bedroom.

I must have sat down because I found myself on my ass, at the foot of my door, sobbing uncontrollably, which must have been when the door to our apartment opened and my mother rushed out, saw me crying at the foot of the door and ran over me, her daughter, kneeing me in the face and hopping down the stairs, hoping to get far away from the apartment which was now very clearly set on fire. So I wailed, and by this time I must be honest, at what I wailed I was not completely certain, it just seemed like it had been such a bad week, what with my father moving next door and then the adopting of the alley cat which ended up not being an alley cat at all and just yesterday with what little sleep I got because of said faux cat problem.

That was when, as I lay on the ground losing blood, the once trusted to be domesticated feline but now understood to be dangerous, enfeebled gypsy rushed in, from God knows where, perhaps coming from the same alley where we found him, waiting for some other unsuspecting family using his same mewing and whimpering. He rushed in and proceeded to nab whatever was within arms reach, ran back out and over my weakened body with towels, Tupperware, anything your standard vagabond would want from a family who had trusted, attempted to nurse with milk and kibble back to a healthy state of being. And there is me now utterly crushed, fetal positioned, crying now not just because of my garish elbow and my apartment's burning but also because of the theft of my favorite parakeet plushy, the one that my father had bought me when I was six, the one that I gave up 2 other toys for in order to have that one and only that one because that one was so expensive. And when I saw that I fell, very hard inside, like my stomach was bottomless. That no matter how much one could love, cat or human or whatever it may be, that no matter how nice the groomer or how expensive the treats were, that subject could and ultimately would turn on you.

I crawled slowly, more slid, down the stairs and onto

the concrete alley where the man had left our couch for later stealing and lurched myself onto said couch to ensure its safety.

It was then that my father came out from our neighbor's back porch with said neighbor not far behind. One arm around the waist of the other and the other, my father, exclaiming, looking for answers. I remember calling my father over with one curled and bloodied finger and telling him all, telling him the truth, that that which was the cause of all of this, this misfortune and tragedy that had befallen us was due to him and his neglect. To which my father replied, how could I forget, he said that a tragedy such as this, why it was random, a terrible situation and that he had only just happened upon it and how could he have caused his sole daughter, the love of his life, this misfortune? I remember our neighbor getting upset, saying something like, what's that you just said pussy cat? And I remember my father turning to my neighbor, consoling him, letting him know he loved him, kissing him, and me, me a mere husk. The neighbor getting upset and yelling at my father and saying, "Choose, choose, choose." And my father cooing and mewing saying, "Don't you worry your pretty little head. Not ever something you would need to worry your pretty little head about darling," as my blood seeped into our brand new couch. And that's when I knew, I knew that that man from before would be back, he would be back for my couch, he would be back for my body, and no one, not even own my father, would stop him.

I LEARNED THAT AUSCHWITZ WAS...

"I learned that Auschwitz was a really good person in school today."

"Ooh did you hear that Stou?"

"He saved a lot of Jewish people from the Holocaust," I said.

"That's very interesting did you hear that Stou?"

"Hm?" said Stou.

"How this man Auschwitz saved a lot of the Jews during the Holocaust," my mother said.

"Uhu," I said. "And Hitler was bad. Sometimes, we learned that he made the Jewish people pee and poo in a big big pile in the middle of huge camps."

"In the middle of camps Stou," said Mom.

"They'd all line up naked and they'd start to pee in the pile and if they had to they'd poo. Then, then they'd eat food but it wasn't good food so our teacher, said the food made them poo a lot. And that, like, the pile would get so big and smelly!" I laughed. "In the middle of the camp there was a big pile of poo!"

"Oh Carol it's not funny to joke about the Holocaust. Who taught you that?" asked Stou.

"I'm only telling you what the teacher told me," I said.

"Tell us more about Auschwitz." She said. "He sounds like such a wonderful man huh Stou?" Mom poked with her fork.

"He had a list and he kept the list so all the people on it were saved. He kept them in secret places so the Nazis couldn't find them. Our teacher said the Nazi's brain washed all the Germans except for Auschwitz."

"That's true," said Mom.

"The Nazi's said they would build a better world but that was a lie."

"We all lie, sweety," said Stou.

"Stou put down the steak for a moment and listen to your daughter."

"I'm listenin and it's nearly givin me a heart attack."

"You don't lie do you Dad?" I asked.

Mom gave Dad a smile and a look.

"Course not sweety," said Stou.

"I haven't had my dessert," I said.

The mother brought the bowl of bananas and strawberries out.

"We need to talk at some point Stou," said the mother. "Whatever this is, this…"

Stou put his hand on his wife's. "We're all trying to make it work honey."

"I don't lie if that's what you're wondering," I said. "The teacher said Hitler was really bad."

"Now I'm not going to get into this with you Martha. This is grown up talk but I will, and this is a promise, I will tell you all about it tonight," said Stou.

I looked up from my dessert. "I made an A+ on my chemistry experiment today."

"I didn't take chemistry," said Stou. "When are they going to teach you about communists sweetie?"

I shrugged.

"I think that's next year," said Mom.

"How would you know?" asked Stou.

She shrugged.

"I think the communists were bad," I said.

Dad patted my head and said, "It's time for bed."

I went up to my bedroom. Held my teddy bear. Curled up. The door opened a crack. I looked at the door wide eyed.

"Coming," I said. I went to the bathroom and brushed my teeth. I looked at myself in the mirror. I tried smiling. I tried smiling bigger. I pumped out my hips with a stern face. I looked at my pretty blonde hair. I'm told I sleep pretty with my teddy bear. I curled up in bed with it. But my eyes were open. I was waiting. Waiting. Waiting. I stood up. Crept to my parent's bedroom.

"It's been a while Stou," said Mom.

"I've been so tired of loving you so much Caroline," Dad said. "I've put my whole weight into loving you and what do I get in return?"

"Don't be so dramatic Stou," she said. "We always have our daughter." She put her arm on his shoulder.

I ran back to bed. It was my only happy part of the night and I waited for it. But no one came. My face was so red. I was so angry.

Next morning Stou was eating in the kitchen.

"It is getting late and you missed the train buster," I said to him.

He kneeled in front of me.

"The train has just arrived," he said. He leaned in

close and kissed me passionately on the lips. I parted his brown gelled hair down the middle just like Alfalfa and The Little Rascals. I put my arms around his neck.

"Don't forget about me. I'll be home tonight," Stou said.

"You're an impossible man to forget Mr. Conrad," I said.

BEING ALONE

I masturbated on Sherman Alexie's Pulitzer-Prize Winning *The Absolutely True Diary of a Part-Time Indian* because I wanted to know what it felt like to be intimate with something great. All of my lovers have been less than fantastic. Nothing ever happens. But Sherman Alexie's book once masturbated on put a resonating tone in my heart. I have no pity for people. I'm just so boring but I figured if I could be close to something that had been close to people maybe something would change.

Perhaps it was the wine or the whisky or the two shots of tequila. Maybe the beers that never seem to leave my belly no matter how many times I pee. Maybe it was all of that, because when I finished and I looked at the book, well, I didn't recognize its greatness. I turned my gaze away in disgust. I had wandering thoughts. How did I get here in Tokyo? Why is my apartment so much larger than others? Why do people say it's expensive to live here? I felt completely alone in my wealth. I will never know what normal problems are. You know what's sad? Is that I'm sad that I'm so lucky. I'm ashamed. I

wanted to wipe the entire slate clean. To start over somewhere else as someone I didn't hate so much.

I go next door, I don't knock. I slide into the bed
beside her. I suppose she is sleeping or wants to be left
alone. I like to be left alone and consoled at the same
time. I like to cry in front of people I respect. She's not
good looking. She doesn't have a good body, but she
bathes and takes care of herself. She is very conscious of
her looks. This is a good thing. I bury my head in her
shoulder blades, where her spine is, and try to forget.
But the beer is sloshing and I have a stomach ache. I tell
myself I just have to survive here for an hour, maybe less
till the pain leaves.

I wake up because she woke up and has to go to
school.

"When did you get here?"

"I woke you up last night."

"No, you didn't."

"Yes, you woke up. I saw your head look up at me for
a second."

"I must have been sleeping."

"But I saw you see me."

"I have to change," she says.

I nod and walk out. My room is a bit messier than
usual. The books from the bookshelf are scattered on the
floor. The book. I go over to it and inspect the damage. A
stain on the cover, dried. How long before I have to leave
this room? I could try and stay in as long as possible. I
could shut the curtains and hide in here until something
must be done. The world always catches up with me
though. There's never a day of no obligation. I must eat
or I must exercise or I must pee and it's all very tiring
because all I really want to do is nothing for a day or so.
But I get away with as much as I can.

I get in bed and fall asleep. Nothing happens in Tokyo. People say things happen here but the clubs are always empty. No one knows what good music is. No one knows how to have a decent conversation. All the women want to be approached, but they'll never go home with you. In clubs all the men are checking how others are listening to the music. They dance the way they think is optimal.

But I can get away with it. A few hours. No one is counting when I show up. I can skip out on exercising. I think of what my ex-girlfriend would have said. She would have broken up with me by now again. She had no mercy for my weaknesses. I sleep. The world spins. The world gets hotter.

Tomorrow is never coming. I rest and relax my eyes. Tonight will though. The café will come into view. Its orange and brown colors—its plain and empty second floor. Maybe I will go to the café and people will be crying. They'll have coffees in their hands and they'll be calling their friends. "The world is changing," they'll say. "We didn't think it was possible but things are changing." And can you tell me why they are crying?

As I go under, I slip into a dream easily. There is the person I want for an agent. "It's a fantastic book," he's saying. "Yes, I'd like you to be my agent," I say. "I want you to be my agent!" But he's saying it's too late. He's changed and found a different book he likes even more. I'm certain if I keep repeating the same words over and over he'll change his mind. "Yes, yes," he's saying, "but it's no good."

It's 8pm but I stay in bed until I finally *feel* like I want to leave. I don't get up if I don't have to. I just wait until I'm ready. That's what all of this is. I try to be good. I try to improve myself. Sleeping is the last vice I have, and I will hold onto it for as long as possible. The days transform things little by little.

I want things now. Now now now like a child. Can I understand? How many people have reached this point before me? How far I will go in the future and how many will have reached that point as well?

The café is almost empty. I look around and see people talking and drinking. The subway passes outside the window. Christmas lights are up outside. People want to be seen. They want to be understood. People want the ones they respect to pat them on the head, say good job. You did good, really. I'm not joking. You're just, you're just fantastic and beautiful and never change.

LET US DANCE A BIT LONGER

And Mom puts her arm around my neck. She says, let's have a dance before Darryl gets home. And she puts on Cream, her favorite band, Cream. And she puts on the song In the White Room. And we dance. In the white room, with black curtains, near the station. I tell her this is my favorite song. Mumzy says this is a great song but have I heard Tom Petty. I tell her no, none of the students at school listen to Tom Petty. But a lot of the boys at school listen to Led Zepplin. She says she doesn't have Led Zepplin. I tell her to put on Tom Petty. Tom Petty comes on and I don't like him. Because I feel safe I tell Mumzy I don't like Tom Petty. Let's listen to Guns N Roses. And she frowns. She doesn't like Guns N Roses. I say, Al Green. I say let's listen to Al Green. And she says OK, I love Al Green.

And I ask, "Mumzy do you have Grateful Dead?" And she, Lizzy, scrunches her face and says, "No." So I jump on her bed and we listen to in the white room with black curtains near the station. And on the radio comes forth the song, in the white room near the station. Cream is now my favorite band. I say, "Lizzy Cream is now my favorite band." And she goes, "But all the cool boys like "Zepplin" don't they? Why don't I go to the store tomorrow and buy "Zepplin" and we can listen to "Zepplin" tomorrow instead?" And I say, "Ooo Lizzy I want to listen to Al Green one more time." And so Al Green comes onto the speakers and he says let's make love, all night long, until the sun goes down. And I say, this sounds like a country song. And my Mumzy already has her nose scrunched up and is saying, this isn't Al Green.

"But you put on Al Green," I say.

"I know I did. I thought I did." And she looks at the CD that is in the music station and she goes, "This isn't Al Green."

And I look at the CD that she took out of her music station and I see it isn't Al Green. And I say, "Ooo Mumzy please play us some Al Green. It's getting late and I want to enjoy Al Green before Darryl comes home."

Mumzy looks at her watch and says, "It's not late. It's only 8pm."

And I say, "Ooo Mommy I thought it was midnight. Let's play something upbeat to go along."

And me and Mumzy jig. Me and Mumzy jig a wild beat. The kind of jig where you lightly wiggle your hips side to side. It is fun. I have a good time. Mumzy is especially good. While we jig, not facing each other, I say, "Look at Lizzy go." She does it slow and with a stern look on her face. I say, "Mummy Lizzy is really moving," I also have a stern look on my face. I jig very fast for a split second and then I say, "Now we're both jigging...now Stop." I throw my hands to the side and we both stop right as the song ends.

I relax on her bed out of breath. She comes over to

me and kisses my lips. "It's early," she says looking at me. "And I don't have any Led Zepplin. But I'll go to the store tomorrow and I'll buy Led Zepplin and I'll go to the store tomorrow and buy Grateful Dead. But for now let's just listen." She falls back on her bed like she is looking at a great expansive sky and says, "This is the best night ever."

"If only Al Green was here," I say looking up at the same imaginary sky.

She smiles. Exhales. And says, "I knew him. He was a great man. The best musician who ever lived."

"Was he tall?" I ask.

"He was."

"Was he sweet?"

"It depended on his mood," says Mumzy. She mangles my hair with her fingers.

"It's getting late," I say. "We should put on Al Green to ease us to sleep."

"It's only 8pm," she says. "Besides, nobody else in our house is asleep. It would be strange to go to sleep before the others. They love everyone you love except for Al Green because they don't like sleeping and they don't like feeling tired. They stay up all night listening to Cream or Bruce Springsteen and when they don't they listen to Tom Petty talk about the American Highway."

I look at my fingers while I play with my fingers.

"The whole time nobody sleeps and dreams about being on the road," she says. "Do you like it when I teach you things?"

I nod.

"Lizzy has a lot of things to teach many people but you," she boops my nose, "are my favorite student."

"I always did well in school even though it wasn't very fun," I say.

"Me too," she says. "You can still learn outside of school."

"I hated school."

"Yes, it's boring it's true," Mumzy shrugs her shoulders.

"Did you like school?"

"Oh yes, I was very good at school and I went every day. If you want to go you should. Do you like me?" she asks.

I nod.

"So tell me, what do you like about me?"

"Pretty."

"I find you handsome."

"Sexy," I say.

"That's a playful thing to say. Who taught you that word?"

"Otis Redding," I say.

"I never played you Otis Redding," she says.

"We listened to it earlier today."

"Wasn't that The Four Seasons?" she asks.

"It was Otis Redding. I know because you said, "I really like Otis Redding," and then you played him.

"I recall something like that," she says absent mindedly. "Anyways, Otis Redding was a great singer."

"Yeah," I say relaxing. "Is there any way we could look at the moon and the stars tonight?"

"They aren't out tonight unfortunately."

"That's a silly thing to say," I say.

"It's true. Some nights they don't come out."

"That's a funny thing to say."

"You're too smart for your own good. How old are you again?"

"I'm 12," I say.

"That old?"

"Yeah," I chuckle.

"Well if you're 12 then I'm 22," she says.

"Liar."

"I knew Otis Redding. He was a great man."

"Was he tall?"

"He was very tall," says Mumzy.

SATS

The next week was me penitently waiting for the test while groping my way through High School. Groping teachers, groping classmates, yearning to learn what I was inept at grasping. How they did what they did the way they did it. How the one student who was very smart had good posture and raised his hand straight and high along with his actually knowing the answer. I mimicked the boy but then found that my knowledge was lacking. That there was something else, not just in the behavior of the successful, that needed to be mimicked.

The smartest girl in class being Janus. Janus with blonde hair and blue eyes and a fashion sense which spawned out of thrift stores. Hardly anyone in those days knew what a thrift store was. Janus knew and she also read in literature class with a voice that made the teacher swoon so thereafter it was always Janus who read for us. She stood up straight in the middle of class and her voice swayed with a cadence reserved for professional poets at real poetry readings, ones Janus probably went to in her free time.

And me and my father with money and then it was my birthday with my father paying money to a musician to play at my birthday. I learned Janus was dating Peter and Peter was a cool kid and he got the famous musician to play at his home for free. And that made me feel really bad. I was very sad about that. Because I felt like a loser and I thought there was some way I could be with Janus, perhaps propositioning her in the rain at the top of my father's grotto because Janus liked the rain.

I was invited by Peter to go to his house to see the artist I had just seen and paid for and all of my friends were going and they knew my father had paid for him and they knew Peter had paid nothing while I had spent so much on the artist. Upon arriving it was clear that the artist was less enthusiastic about being at Peter's house perhaps because Peter's sound system was not nearly as good as the professional venue my father had purchased. By the time I got there a lot of people weren't dancing.

Peter and Janus were on the hanging lawn chairs behind the pool and I heard someone say did you hear? That Peter was fingering Janus, and I knew it was true because Peter got what he wanted. I went to the trampoline and said Hi to everyone and they were all nice, one was a girl and two were guys and they asked if I wanted some marijuana. I said sure I did. They asked me where I was from and what school I went to and when I answered I could tell they listened and they all said cool. I relaxed for a bit on the trampoline and listened to them talk about existence and freedom.

Soon the marijuana rose within me and I felt emboldened. I felt more aggressive and all around more of a decisive person. I said excuse me and told them I would be back. I walked over to the pool where the lawn chair was and I went over to the lawn chair where Janus was and they were smiling as if there was something amusing right in front of them.

"What's up?" said Peter laughing.

"Not much," I said.

"OK," said Peter laughing with Janus and I wondered if they were laughing at me.

"I was just listening to the band," I said. "My father has a lot of musician friends. I can introduce you sometime." I wasn't looking at Peter anymore. I was looking at the darkness of the night and even though it was the city I saw a few scattered stars just over Peter's backyard fence. But I wasn't really looking at that either. I was looking back at Peter but not really looking at him. I felt like such a fool but my mind was the controller of my thoughts and I didn't let anything make me feel like a fool.

"Cool," I said. "Your party is pretty cool."

"Yeah, OK," said Peter. "Bye." He laughed with Janus.

"I'll introduce you to some of my friends," I said. "They're really great musicians and you'd be interested in their thoughts."

"Sounds good."

"You can meet my father too. He's really cool," I said.

"OK."

"Bye," I said and started to leave but then I looked at Peter and I said, "I think you're really cool. You're really lucky to be who you are with Janus and all of that you're a really good musician."

My father always told me to be kind and always be especially kind to those who are cruel. That the cruel are weak and Jesus is strength. That's what my father said. My father also told me once, "If you ever get into trouble just stay positive." As I walked away the feeling was my heart was beating really fast and my focus was on whatever my eyes were looking at. I looked back at them with the courage the marijuana had given me and I wondered if there would be any doubt in Peter's behavior or maybe Janus would be looking sad over the way Peter had treated me but I don't think she did. I walked back to the backyard where the trampoline was and I heard laughter. Another thing my father taught me was to always go towards the ones who give you affection. So I went up to the trampoline and I asked if I could join them.

FEEL SOMETHING BIG

There are times. Yes, there are times. He feels so filled up he no longer finds something big. There are things. Yes, there are things. In himself and he finds something big. There are times yes many times, when he finds something in himself worth pursuing. During these times. Yes during these very specific times, he holds on.

During these times. Yes during these momentous times. He understands the humility involved in the pressure.

During the weight. The weight which closes in. He no longer feels big and the crushes feeling like a feeling.

But sometimes he feels it. Sometimes he feels something big. Yes the exploring is endless yes I have said it before, there is no path that is not open to him.

And so he comes here. The point of no longer wanting. He is too big to follow those who came before. When he is this big. There are no ways to follow from those who came before. When he is this, and the paths are so endless, he no longer follows those who came before. This dangerous. This no longer wanting. This so many ways. This many options are many options so many.

SALARYMEN4

Salary men were scared but then less so. It was good it got less. More terror is never an answer. Unless you count Quintin who thrives off it. You're doing great! A little mask I did wear to not contract a virus in the 2020 year. The year reminded me of a smell. A bird is for squeaking and, I have one, and that is a good thing for everyone. Especially the salarymen who I'll be getting to shortly, briefly, almost insanely dilatory, dilatorily? Because more to the point, and there is a point, with which we want to make, I want to make, and so do you once you hear it, that there are some insane layers involved here in this story before we ever come to really understand that "arriving" is a kind of seeing. Mastery. Intellectual pursuits. Redemption. A way of being in the world. So yes, I know, I will get to your aforementioned story but before all of that, have you seen me? I mean really looked in the mirror and in the eyes, mine or your own and really seen me? Or are we not arriving quite yet? Because the truth is, to be frank with you, I have come too far to really be slowly pulling your weight across this thing. It is really a beautiful thing, this is, and we'd all do well to enjoy it. If you think I am going to, nay want to, pull you towards something which only those of us can reach with a very kind of, a weakening in the attention to the, a wild but subdued desire for, if you think you can't let yourself...

Before we continue on this uh, story, let's get to more about me. I had a wonderful time playing video games. More about me, I am a part time backgammon player. That is enough about me. Now we will talk more about her.

She is super.

So I like to do this stuff as a freshener so you know who I am and what I want out of you. Now I know some of you are no longer following all of this and now we can truly begin. Now is the time to really start where I wished to from the beginning since I told you I would not carry all of you the whole way. Now that we have lifted some of the pounds, I will begin the story that I originally intended to tell.

When they were younger oh how they were younger wanting something safe and comfortable and that hunger which is an addiction and a good one to have, society thrives just off of that as does man and so does woman a hunger for safety in the older age one wants something else. Every single time anyone receives any single thing they ever wanted they do seem to turn away from don't they. Don't they? The salarymen were kind of certain seductive about what they were doing, it was late but I knew at least one of them should have been and their attitudes. Confidence is attractive to some but not all, a certain woman wants a man low. This one. In the corner. But for some a crying for a woman is usually a turn off though I do suppose a turn on the older more mature for some. One does find the older the more love they enjoy love.

The question of course comes back to me, a 30 year old writer, but certain fantasy still coming into himself. Certainly I would wonder with a whisper, about me writing a salaryman in his forties from Tokyo.

But pontificate to the Park Hyatt Bar with the low lighting and the single lit lantern in the corner bar where a man sits with a tequila, no matter feminine, with a woman in a bright red dress that shines, perfectly strong jaw in the light. The rest of the bar all in black. A ready man's hands ready to catch the gin. All nice and choreographed we have a rhythm to that very scene, what you have is a choice is fine. I see it you may read it, probably will actually, that it's fine either way.

A man in a chair or a woman on a bed, the same thing. Different places. I was taken to the more I wrote. Interchanging then realizing what they were doing. A man in a bed and a woman in a bed. Two in a bed at the Park Hyatt Bar. And it was the bar. There were women and there were men and they were having intercourse. A sex, a good time, fun time, at the Park Hyatt Bar never mind their living. Situation. A situation occurs with a man in a bar in a red dress and a woman in a bar with a cocktail in hand. The hand a maneuver around the glass. A glass a hand a feeling.

A glass. A corner. A story. A corner story. A corner cornered in a room. An angle in the room. That one bird outside the room. What did it have to do to see its way to these heights at the top of the bar with a man and a woman in a bar making love on the 31st floor of this Park Hyatt Bar in the center of Tokyo I did once go, the first time I ever went to Tokyo with my ex-girlfriend named Allison. But a different story same timing, a man in a drink and a woman in bed, both falling flailing enjoying themselves. For a night. A whisper. A watch can be expensive. But just watch how this man's hands, do curl around, the back of her waist. It feels refreshing. To watch.

The Communal Pool the next day a boy and his father played. They went and did have fun. Watching the children go, Modern Day of course. Modern Inflatables, exhaling elastic buzzing words, Hey, Come here! Come over here! Did you see what that just happened over there! I started swimming! Said the son. Personally, the author, he swam at 9 months old no father needed.

Just so the women chose their wanderlust husbands slowly growing second thumbs but they still loved them and it doesn't at all effect their work, the salarymen, and doesn't effect their talk, the women wives, and also for some reason does effect children in Nicaragua. I will get to how that another time, I will also get to how the husbands feel about their extra opposable thumbs a moment from now, but talking about myself with my own hands hardships though the other for a moment. The Nicaraguan Catastrophe should be mentioned, of course it should, be noted, as a Catastrophe, a Travesty but this is too depth for the purpose essays like this one unfortunate. This one unfortunate, ugly unfortunate for a story, but perhaps necessary to get across something? Extra thumbs no one wants to read but perhaps important for the purpose of conveying just how husbands feel about what it is that is occurring? Anyways, too depth for the article of this enjoyment. For the wives were at the café discussing forest fires, great large great heaping hoops of forest fires ravaging the bellows of the Japanese countryside living feeling little smaller people burning alive, but not them. The wives at the café discussing the husbands at the bar. There were people who watched me go up to the sun and it was really beautiful to experience something like that. They do, they do believe after the years, their husbands will stay and so we end up here at a café.

The salary men were at the Park Hyatt Bar. Their extra thumbs, oh I don't like writing it but, perhaps for the story important? Perhaps necessary to convey a certain feeling? An adult learns to look at it. In the room a dress undone, a boy in the room, pretty happy actually, just to be involved in a fantasy. A happy man. A salary person. Just happy to be involved in someone's character turning off. And then slowly becoming and then showing themselves, in a different place. Kind of far away from the other stuff. Stuff, is a good word if you don't care about it. And then there were others, the one's in the rooms all around the Park Hyatt Bar, doing the same thing, and then oh no, it's getting sad again. A universal theme.

OF INFIDELITY> And now we become our father's, a universal theme. We become the old traditions. OF 2% WINNING CHANCES NONE. WITH 25% WANT. A double. A CUBE. A take. I WANT. A board porcelain and firm. A father porcelain and firm. A buzzing corrupting the porcelain. A son porcelain and firm. A father teaching a son how to be a board. As big as a backgammon board. A porcelain and firm board. A porcelain and firm board. A man in the throes of flourishing. A buzzing. A board porcelain skin. My porcelain skin I a board. Porcelain skin. And buzzing. And yearning.

And the age inherent in yourself. You realize you are still buzzing. And a woman in a red dress does introduce yourself. You realize you are not old. But young, desired, one who lacks substance but perhaps enough of a way in.

A backgammon probability of 9/36 times I win. Before we learned probabilities there was love. And then I got lost somewhere in there But when life is not enough, backgammon is not enough, writing never though enough but pursues the angle of going further into the fantasy, pursuing any line of thinking well, obviously I want it. I remember a probability of 30% in a backgammon passes less often, thinks an advantage but actually I did reach up, up across the board, a big board, a bar in Tokyo, a beautiful bra, backgammon board, 30% winning chances, a big game, a bruiser of books we wrote together one night. I want the red dress and I want the wife and the home. I want to wear a red dress and a home. And sure, sure as certain as I can ever be since romantic love did become a horror story. Gee,

For I did know of one, the author did, Marston Hefner, know an author who, fell in love with a woman. Moved next door to her, creepy but romantic, and then got together with her. One David Foster Wallace. And he did happen to try to throw this woman he loved out of his car, no apologies made. Nothing formally written out to people like us saying, "Gee that was terrible. I'm sorry." He just opened the door, went to throw her out, was like, bye. And then she stayed with him I guess, I don't know why, but then she left, and wrote a book, and became a famous writer. Mary Karr. And so that's something.

Another probability. Another outcome. A decision. An outcome. A forced move. I was the one a conquest. A victory a home. I was the one reaching. A firm hand going. A porcelain bird firm my father's hands held. A father's hands hold. Backgammon board given my father's playing was quintessential for my improvement. A father a board. Touched another. I escaped once a night a home. A wife a home. I loved the one in the story. Where we went for a night away. A drink had. A woman's jaw—thick lined and porcelain Greeks made porcelain boards backgammon fathers became. A simple piece of wood, no different from a story. A creation being made. An artisan. No different from an artist. A craft. No different than an art. I want to, make wood, a backgammon board. As to a father I have none. As to me being a father, I love my wife. For the scornful, I have nothing. For the lovers, growing over ageing. In the end, the database collected, the Greeks did make a board made of white. And it is now in a museum, where a salary man did look with his son, admiring the detail.

BASEBALL

There wasn't any time. As far as I knew there was time. I would object to whatever fucking message this was about. Whether it was about me learning rationality or a sense of duty or a sense of things greater than myself I didn't care I wanted no part of it. I thought the world had taught me enough and it was time for me to teach something to myself.

I missed my hair cut. I'd go later at another time when the world wasn't so pressing time wasn't so pressing the world wasn't so dire in need of my haircut but when I felt comfortable doing it. Then I would go and only then. Until then the world would have to wait, I had flipped it around. I was the one and the world was two and that's it. So I played video games.

Lyrically I'm there but spiritually and structurally you want me further no? Yes. You do. You want me over there but I am here. I have tried going over there but I don't enjoy it. It comes down to that. I want to enjoy myself. Forgive me for the long and the shorts and the boring and the dull it is oh so hard to hit it to you when

I'm over here. Over there? Oh sure over there I could hit it so far right to you and further if you wanted. It is so fun hitting it further from there for sure but you do it for so long and you keep trying to do it over there because the world wants you over there it feels less like that is the place to be the older I get. So I end up here and here is not so great believe me I know. I know it and so do you but what can I do? I am trying to enjoy myself the best I can day after day and being here is so fun some-times it is so fun sometimes but I don't know I get tired here as well.

You deserve it. You deserve it and I'll bring it. You've paid with your money or your time and you deserve something good your life is worse than mine or harder than mine or better than mine it doesn't matter what matters is your time is here and so you deserve a story that sends the ball way over there and beyond because this is your time you're putting into me and I should have something for you who is putting their time into this and

Whether or not whoever is right I sure know I'll give you what you want to give you something good I sure know I will. I don't want to beat around the bush the whole damn time telling you and telling you how hard it is to do it. I don't want to keep trying to get you on my team on this one because this one here is a dull stock still no life to it a corpse and boy do I know it. I know it and so do you. So I'll be clear with you on that. I wouldn't lie and I never cheat that's not in me.

If I had no worry about it it would come true but who the hell knows how to make the worry invisible how to really feel good all the time so they produce that good right there and then there is nothing but quality. Always good and always no worry wow that would be incredible but also patently unhuman and art is always the human and that means bad and terrible things are necessary for the human art is always human and so this bad is so human and so necessary but that doesn't mean I will subject this to you. You don't deserve this or anything like this. So I'll hit it over to you.

But you know how it is. You can't keep going on with the better sometimes you need the worse before the better happens. But soon I'll send that sucker right over the fence I will. You're not going to think I could do it. You think oh there's no way he could send that sucker right over the fence and right into my glove. The accuracy. No one could. The pin striped flannels. Why is he wearing them? He's not an athlete who could do it but I promise you. I swear to God there will be an occurring.

I'm certainly ready. I've gotten just about juiced up and ready to do it. I'm more ready than ever before. I'm ready but are you ready? OK. Don't forget what I told you. I never wanted to be hitting this ball but hit I will and boy that sucker will go flying. Further than you thought. I might just send it over past you, you who is already so far away.

Put a line in the sand. Tell me where you'd like it to go and I'll do it. Go on. Put a line in the sand. Stop dilly dallying you're taking up my time. You're taking too long. Who taught you how to draw a line in the sand? You're doing it like you don't even care.

You know what? You know what's wrong with you? You have no appreciation for what I'm about to do. You don't believe me do you? You don't believe I could do it so you don't even care that I'm about to do it. Well if you don't care you bet your ass I don't care. You bet your ass I won't hit the ball that far.

How can anyone hit the ball as far as you expect with

that look on your face? What is that look? Well buddy you got to care and put a line in the sand before I do anything with this ball before I even start to really think about what it takes to even start myself to get that ball past that goddawful line you just drew.

How can you expect me to do anything with the sorry state you're in? You think me hitting the ball right past where you just drew that line will fix the sorry state you're in? There's nothing I can do with this ball in my hand to fix the sorry state you're in. No matter what I do there's nothing I can do. You know what you are? You're clinically depressed. There's no game in that. There's no fun in that. And I'm playing a game. I can play the game all day long but it can't change that frown of yours, the way you flop your hands the way you do. There's no way for me to win this game you're playing.

I was going to send this sad sucker further than that half hearted line you just drew but now you'll just have to sit with that then. You'll just have to think this over long and hard and ask yourself what you really wanted out of all of this. Whether you just wanted to see someone fail at something.

Yes I think you better ask yourself if maybe what you really wanted to see was me failing to hit this ball over there. I think there is something deeply wrong with what you want my friend. Because what you want is you taking enjoyment out of my failure. You better think about your attitude my friend, before expecting anyone to do anything close to hitting this ball further than you ever thought possible and

FAST FREDDY

As for me, I loved running through the school yard. It was my primal joy and I aimed to be the best at it since I was so terrible at all other things. I put my whole self-worth on it, on top of it, and I was good at it or so I knew when I ran.

But of course there was always Freddy and Freddy was always very fast. Freddy like me couldn't beat the fastest kids in school but he was very fast. He could beat whoever unless it was like Ray or Ashwin. Ray was one grade lower so he didn't count and Ashwin was one of the nicest kids in school so no one really thought about him. It seemed in just about everything Freddy and I were near equals so he was always my natural rival.

One day our PE Coach Lenny said, "How about you two boys race?"

And we agreed of course, both of us wondering who was the fastest. I lined up against Freddy, I put my foot on the line and I hoped that whatever wind would be pushing me through it would push me through it, that mystery when it hit my back and let me know I'd win.

Sometimes I felt it and sometimes I didn't, but when I felt it my muscles relaxed and I'd think "Ahhh this is it and I've found it" but all in kid-speak, back then I didn't have a name for it, the thing that gave me the confidence to race so fast.

"Whoever wins is the fastest kid in school," said our PE Coach Lenny. Then she said, on your marks, get set, go.

And I ran. And Freddy ran too. At first we were tied and then I was ahead. Eventually I was getting even further ahead, making progress on my already good fortune. I was breaking away and the wind it felt like it was pushing my tuchus forward, levitating my feet, making my legs lighter than ever. And I was winning. So long as I kept winning victory was at the end. But that was when I saw Freddy catching up. So I was focusing on Freddy but I was also trying to run faster, then I told myself to just run faster but I couldn't help but focus on Freddy who was catching up with me. I pushed and I pushed. I knew if I pushed harder for three or so seconds I would win. I only had to push harder than Freddy and that was all. If I wanted it more and God knew I wanted it more the race would be over but Freddy was passing me. Freddy was slightly ahead of me and I died inside.

Freddy crossed that finish line and I had stopped just short of it, knowing what I knew there was no point in finishing. It felt like my limbs weren't as capable as Freddy's and my being was less than whatever Freddy's was. I ran more than anyone else in the school but I still couldn't beat Freddy. He was smiling and I smiled back because he was such a good kid and we were friends. He put his hand on my shoulder and said good job but it didn't take much for me to think Freddy was lying. Good job? I had lost and I wasn't even close to the best. Freddy was better than me and there was always Ray and there was always Ashwin. I had put everything, everything that was within me, into a race that I lost, and all of it, all that I pushed into myself, just to be the fourth fastest kid in school.

A SETTING

A luxury is a place. A name to a face. Give her one. Lila.
Which sounds like a diamond. So that will be her name.
She will wear pearls around her neck. A small tight neck
around her bone. There will be orifices touched by a
man. Bob.

An eccentricity. Lila has a home, a good place to stay.
Bob is there. In a corner of the room smoking marijuana.
Lila is calling her father on her cellphone. A cellphone,
modern. A modern thing is sometimes taboo. That is fine
for this story. Nimble on his feet he moved to the bed.
Where Lila is not. And it was not like Bob to move this
way. He often did and he often tries to stop it. Moving
too quickly startling. But Lila remains talking on the
phone not caring. So we know Lila is fine. So I know,
reader, later on she became someone elses. It's said there
should be an apostrophe but Lila surprised me. Lila is a
reader. She didn't mess with Saunders. He didn't really
know what he was doing outside of what he was doing.
That's important to know in terms of Lila and Lila's
living.

"I love you very much," says Lila to her father.

"I love you too, so much."

Now you may know something. There is something perhaps heading in a certain direction that may be considered down. Lila is a happy person. She is strong in herself not despite her childhood. Her father visited her bed and he was welcome there. His hands were always big to her but welcome. He was welcome and then she grew up violent. A testament to his hands is drawn in her algorithm, making their shape when put in the processor. An omen or a cure is a choice when grown up. But what to do when deep down. And he had welcoming hands when she was younger. But as she grew up she started fighting and how I already introduced Bob.

Her mother sits at the table. She is feeling sick as she watches her daughter talk. I think you know who I mean. Lila's mother. Lila's father is talking. He is involved. Lila's leg kicks under the table, wondering if it will find a leg.

"It's been too long," says her father with a glass in the air.

"We're getting old," says Lila. "What are we toasting to?"

"Finding love."

They clink glasses and her mother takes slow sips. Lila sets the glass down.

"It's been a busy holiday."

"That's a shame," says her father.

Lila never really liked Carole but Lila never really liked talking about death either. Carole's face looked pulled back more than before and her lips looked fuller.

"The new found Christian alt right literature presage old testament new thought bundles," says her father.

"Yes," Carole, her mother, says.

"I fell asleep a long time and when I woke up I thought, you know what, I could sleep some more."

"That's progress."

"I was depressed," says her father sitting across from Lila.

"I'll do the dishes," says her mother.

"Why don't I help you?" says her father.

"I'm fine. You two catch up."

Her father's shoulders relax. Lila touches her wine glass with her finger, hoping it would make a sound.

"How's work?"

"Aching," Lila says. "How's California?"

Her father looks away. He looks back at her and says, "Everyone is always hustling and it's exhausting."

Lila looks down at her wineglass and smiles. She laughs and her father laughs too.

"Do you have any girlfriends?" Lila asks.

"It's not in the cards at the moment. We are similar in that regard."

"..."

"It's hard letting someone in once you've been hurt," he says. "But it all works out for the best. I'm not worried about you. I think we should all have the freedom to do more of what we want to do. I mean, we're all adults and productive enough already. When do we actually stop all of this, for a moment?"

"You wouldn't stop though," says Lila. "You would go on sleeping forever."

"No I wouldn't."

"Remember that one time we went camping and you didn't come out of the tent for 3 days?" she says.

"I was depressed."

There is a knock on the apartment door. It is Frank

from down the hall. We notice Frank as the man who owns hamsters, right?

"Do you two have any leftovers?" asks Frank.

"We don't eat really," says Lila. "Please, have some food."

"My hamsters are typically on a vegetable diet, but it's the holidays and they like sugar. I was hoping to procure something sweet for them, a forbidden treat. A Bon Bon or something else that's sweet."

"We don't have dark chocolate Frank," says Lila.

"Is Carole in here?" asks Frank.

"She's doing the dishes."

"..."

One morning I brushed my teeth. Lila came up to me and told me she was pregnant.

"A little child was born today in my bosom but that is open to interpretation," she said.

I kissed her belly. Joy joy joy! I am now a dog.

"I will go anywhere for our child," I say.

She kissed my lips. I kissed her forehead. She fell asleep in the crook of my arm. I fell asleep my head on top of hers. I dreamt of something scary. I dreamt of a jackal in my dreams chasing down something fierce. I worried for my safety. When I woke up I didn't worry any longer. When I woke up the sun was shining in front of the open sun. I walked outside and went to work on a puzzle of a dog.

I was born a baby. A baby became a man a man became a saint. A saint has nowhere to go from there. I was born a baby. I was worried when I was 18-20 but that ceased. I was controlled chaos as a teenager until I couldn't anymore. Until my brain gave up and got older.

A normal way of living was not interesting to me but

no one told me that the darkness likes to touch the outside of your skin, so light but still there.

The more I run the older I get the more I brake for my chosen friends. The more I take the time to give some love to them. The stronger I get the scareder I get that fallen won't come back to success. This is a success story so don't mind the needles. OH THE NEEDLES EXIST.

When I wake up I write in the morning and then I read and promising. Never quite reaching the top of any of it I assume a man is in a room training twice as hard as I am. These are the ones who go further than me. They are often less kind than me but they don't care much I assume I hardly know. I don't talk to them if that's what you're wondering.

In the woods I searched. Found more promising in the night. It was easier once I got older. When I was younger it was scary.

I watch horror movies. If someone is feeling this way I am joyful. There are so many lights out there it is the afternoon. The sun can't help itself. T

The sun was bright. Overcoming with confidence in the children of today. Brains like wow, have a seat and listen to daddy speak.

You're all too overconfident. Humble yourself until you reach an age where you can think reasonably.

A stack of nails. A flower in a yard. I choose the flower. Why would I do different One is ugly and one is pretty. There, that is art!

I am a dog. I am a cat. I am a monster. Let me in. Hey honey I'm at the door let me in. Marston Monster is at your door. Let me in hey! I don't want to hurt no one any more.

A FAMILY HISTORY

My father took his women his young women outside, he did not take us his children my brother and I to the sports games. My father did not want to talk anymore about any possibility of his children seeking things that were my father's from the outside. His power and his fame, my father already did not like giving his power and his fame to the young women in his life. My father thought his children wanted what he did not want to give, but we all know this is not what children want a father to give, no it is not the outside children yearn for. My father did not know a father can give his children a secret power in something inside themselves so simple from a sports game between one father and two sons. A father and two sons can come together from something so simple as this and gain a power from a father giving something inside his children a secret power within them just like their father had his secret power within him.

My mother did not want to give. My mother let others give to her what was difficult for her to have. Her strength was in knowing how to tell others what to give, in demanding what others do what was too difficult for her. Her strength was receiving and this is a strength sometimes because others believe that is so. That my mother had the right to receive so and so. My mother did not give anything but to her children. Her children she gave everything.

My father did not give love to anyone but my mother. He was not only quiet but strong in his receiving from others his young women. He never expected anything but everything. He was a man, he never wanted anything that gave to others. He was a man, he never wanted love given to his children. My father only gave love to his wife. It was an honor for his wife to receive, she was with a man who gave nothing but everything to her. This is how my father learned sacrifice. He gave to one thing and always one thing and everything in one thing. His sacrifice was this and he taught his children to sacrifice nothing but this.

Over time his wife my mother did not wish to receive. We are forgetful, a great many people in love do forget the things they receive. We are forgetful. A very many people are forgetful of the many things their husbands and wives give to them. No matter how special the giving it happens. Many times a husband or wife is very kind in giving but the other is forgetting. The forgetting happens with all sorts of people from all walks of life, no matter how important one husband is to his wife, the forgetting happens very often anyways.

Many of the videos I watched with me as a child with my brother as a baby contain my mother looking elsewhere and my father looking at her while my mother looking elsewhere with my father looking at her. My father gave his love for it was his only love and if one has only one love it has to be everything. My mother did not like being given everything, my mother did not want only this everything given to her with so much sacrifice and so she began her forgetting.

There is a great lesson here. There are a many great lessons here but the one lesson I know is one's power must always be more than one thing. My mother's only power was her beauty. My mother having only one power started her forgetting. My mother's only power was a reason for my father's giving. My mother's only power started her divorcing.

My father his children his children wondered how to make their father proud of them and full of wonder just the way their mother had made in him, her husband so full of wonder. In a room in his mansion was my father his children wondering how to make their father give everything to them, they asked him in his room, how could they make him full of wonder the way their mother had made in him. My father thought his children wanted money and fame. My father did not know his children wanted loving and awe. His children that was me and my brother, never made their father look at them with the same feeling. It was not the same feeling when he saw his children. It was not a secret feeling kept inside him.

Because the wind was hitting me, my father not giving me, he did not make me cold when he hit inside of me, disappointed me. He did not make me cold. The wind hit inside of me. The wind shook me. I will say it again. My father did not make me cold, did not shake me the way the wind shook inside of me. Did not stop. I am not my father. My life within me I trust the feelings inside me. One more thing, I let the feelings inside me.

PREVIOUSLY PUBLISHED

My Special Creature was previously published by "Juked Magazine".

IM DONE DELLILO was previously published by "Back Patio Press".

High School Romance was previously published by "Hobart Pulp".

The Kind Of Like, Running Motion Towards Something was previously published by "Gay Death Trance".

You and Me and Like, where do we go after all this time? and *Being Alone* was previously published by "Tyrant Magazine".

A Family History was previously published by "Black Telephone".

ACKNOWLEDGMENTS

Thank you to my publisher Christoph Paul who is not just a business partner but a best friend. He believed in me when other bigger presses didn't and I believed in CLASH just the same. I love you Christoph. I want to thank my therapists Ron and Lee. Both of you helped me understand my genius, that my deviance from the norm is not weak or shameful but my strength. Most of all I am grateful for Anna Lambropoulos who loved the 'darkest' parts of me throughout the entirety of our relationship. Every aspect of you is genuine.

ABOUT THE AUTHOR

Marston Hefner is the editor and founder of Young Magazine, a professional backgammon player, and has published work in New York Tyrant. Born and raised in Los Angeles, he prefers staying in, playing videogames, and reading over the nightlife and the glamor. Marston Hefner continues the legacy Hugh Hefner left him, exploring sexual taboos, finding radical self-love in humanity's darkest unconscious desires.

ALSO BY CLASH BOOKS

WE PUT THE LIT IN LITERARY

clashbooks.com

FOLLOW US

TWITTER

IG

FB

@clashbooks

EMAIL

clashmediabooks@gmail.com

CPSIA information can be obtained
at www.ICGtesting.com
Printed in the USA
JSHW030527111122
32865JS00003B/3

9 781955 904056